"Smasher!" screamed Mrs. Buzzard. "You bad dog, you!"

She stood up and grabbed a mop and aimed a furious blow at the puppy, a blow that broke the remaining jam jars even as she slipped on the wet floor and fell flat on her back.

When she got to her feet once more, Smasher was nowhere to be seen.

"Only meself to blame," grumbled Mrs. Buzzard as she went down the passage to shut the back door.

"And you can stay out!" she shouted down the yard as she closed it. "Should have had more sense than to let you in in the first place."

Smasher, however, was still in the house.

SMASHER

By **Dick King-Smith**

Illustrated by **Richard Bernal**

SCHOLASTIC INC.

New York   Toronto   London   Auckland   Sydney
Mexico City   New Delhi   Hong Kong   Buenos Aires

ISBN-13: 978-0-439-50320-4
ISBN-10: 0-439-50320-5

12 11 10 9 8 7 6 5 4 3 2 1   7 8 9 10 11 12/0

Printed in the U.S.A.   40

First Scholastic printing, March 2007

Contents

1

The Ugly Puppy

"Kindest thing I could do for you," said Farmer Buzzard, "would be to knock you on the head."

He stood in the stable looking down into a shallow wooden box filled with straw, where his collie Kay lay nursing her litter of newborn puppies.

He was not talking to Kay, though she wagged her tail at the sound of his voice.

He was not talking to three of the four

puppies, who were all black-and-white miniatures of their mother.

He was talking to the fourth puppy.

The fourth puppy looked nothing like the others. It was bigger, it was the color of milky coffee, and it had a very large, blunt head with a wrinkled face. It looked, in short, like a freak.

Farmer Buzzard bent down and picked up the fourth puppy in one large hand and held it in front of his face.

"Good thing your eyes is closed, my son," he said to it. "Because if you was to catch sight of yourself in a mirror, you'd have a fit, you would. I never seed anything so ugly in all my born days. You're not going to be no use to no one. I got to do away with you. I'll be doing you a favor, I will."

As though she could understand his words, Kay whined softly.

"All right, all right," said Farmer Buzzard. "Keep him for now, old girl." He put the fourth puppy back with the rest and walked out of the stable.

In the kitchen of the farmhouse, Mrs. Buzzard had breakfast ready. As some married couples do, the Buzzards looked strangely alike, so that they might have been taken for brother and sister. Both were tall and angular with strong, curved noses. Strangers sometimes thought them well named, so much did they call to mind a pair of big birds of prey. Oddly, Mrs. Buzzard had been a Miss Hawk before she married.

Now she said, as she had said every mealtime for the past thirty years, "Wash your hands."

Farmer Buzzard washed them. As he stood drying them, he said, "Kay's whelped."

"How many pups?" asked Mrs. Buzzard.

"Four."

"All right, are they?"

"Three are. Look just like Kay."

"What's up with t'other?"

"Martha," said Farmer Buzzard solemnly, "he's the ugliest puppy you ever did see. Who the father of them is I do not know, but to see this puppy you'd think his dad was the Hound of the Baskervilles. I shall have to knock him on the head."

Mrs. Buzzard smiled. She knew how tender-hearted her husband was. She put a plate of bacon and eggs in front of him and said, "Eat your breakfast, Ken, and then you can go and put the poor little creature out of his misery. A little runt, is he?"

"No," said Farmer Buzzard. "He's the biggest."

"Weakly, then?"

"No, the strongest."

"Just ugly?"

"Aye," said Farmer Buzzard. "Ugly as sin."

"Dear, dear," said Mrs. Buzzard.

At the end of the morning, when her husband came in for his midday meal, she said, "Done it, then?"

"Done what?" said Farmer Buzzard.
"Put that puppy down."
"Oh, no, I forgot. Been that busy."

In the afternoon, Mrs. Buzzard went out with
a bucket of corn and a basket to feed her
hens and collect their eggs. On her way back

she went into the stable to see Kay and her litter. The three black-and-white puppies were all asleep, full fed, but the big brown puppy was still nursing busily. The look of pride on the collie's face told Mrs. Buzzard just what the mother thought of her hideous pup.

"Don't you fret, my girl," she said to the dog. "Farmer Buzzard won't never harm him. He's too soft."

That evening after tea she said to her husband, "Treat yourself to a glass of beer, I should. 'Twill make you feel better. It must have been a hard thing to do."

"Feel better?" said Farmer Buzzard. "Hard thing? What are you on about?"

"Killing that puppy, of course."

Farmer Buzzard grinned sheepishly.

"I didn't," he said.

"Whyever not?"

"Not his fault he looks like he does. You never know, he might get better-looking when he's growed."

"Can't fail to," said Mrs. Buzzard.

"You know what, Martha?" said her husband. "I think I'll have that glass of beer. You like anything?"

"I shouldn't mind a drop of port," said Mrs. Buzzard. When her husband had fetched the glasses, she said, "We'll drink to his health, shall we?"

"What, that puppy?"

"Yes. And he ought to have a name, now that you've decided to keep him."

"Don't know about keeping him," said Farmer Buzzard. "I shall be selling all the puppies once they're old enough."

"Reckon anyone will want him? Seeing he's so ugly? Perhaps that's what we'd better call him. 'Ugly.' After all, even if he does improve in looks, he's never going to be a smasher, is he?"

"'Smasher!'" said Farmer Buzzard. "That's it! That's what we'll call him!" And they touched glasses and drank.

2

Chicken Chasing

Eight weeks later, Farmer Buzzard put an advertisement in the local paper, which read:

COLLIE PUPPIES FOR SALE,
TWO MALES, ONE FEMALE.
FROM GOOD WORKING MOTHER.
STEADY ON SHEEP OR CATTLE.

When Mrs. Buzzard read it, she said, "I see you've only advertised three."

"That's right," said her husband.

"Well, well," said Mrs. Buzzard.

Over the next few days, several people came to look at the puppies. The first was another farmer, a neighbor of the Buzzards, and he knew exactly what he wanted.

"I'll have the female puppy, Ken," he said. "I've always fancied having a daughter of your Kay's. She's a good un, she is."

He squatted on his heels and patted the three black-and-white pups.

"Nice level lot," he said. "Who's the father?"

"Oh, you wouldn't know him," said Farmer Buzzard.

At that moment Smasher, who had been playing by himself in a far corner of the stable, came bumbling up. He pushed his smaller brothers and sister out of his way and licked the neighbor's hand with his large, slobbery tongue.

"What's this, then?" said the neighbor. "He's not out of the same litter, is he?"

Farmer Buzzard nodded. "Throwback," he said.

"Throwback!" said the neighbor. "I reckon I'd have thrown him *out*."

He looked at the brown puppy, noting the size of his feet and the folds of loose skin on his big face.

"He's more like a bull-mastiff than a collie," he said. "What an object! However did your Kay come to have one like that?"

"Dunno," said Farmer Buzzard.

"Ain't *he* ever ugly!" said the neighbor. When there was no reply to this, he added, "Well, he's no beauty, Ken, is he?"

"Not pertickerly," said Farmer Buzzard.

"You going to keep him?"

"Dunno. I might."

The second man to come in search of a puppy was obviously nearsighted. He wore a pair of thick spectacles. And when he was shown the three remaining puppies, he pointed straight at Smasher and said, "I'll have the brown one."

For a split second Farmer Buzzard was tempted. Here was the one chance of a home for the ugly puppy (which he didn't need to keep—Kay did all the work of the farm with no trouble). Nobody but a half-blind man would have picked him.

The farmer looked at Smasher's large, wrinkled face, turned up to him with a sort of grin on it.

"Sorry," he said. "The brown un's not for sale. There's two other puppies to pick from."

"You choose one of them for me, then," said the nearsighted man. "My sight's not so good these days. Pity about the brown one, though. A fine-looking little chap, from what I can tell."

That same day the other black-and-white puppy was sold to another farmer, and Smasher was left alone with his mother.

That night as he lay beside her in the stable, he said, thoughtfully, "I don't look much like you, Mum, do I?"

Kay surveyed her remaining child. Poor little chap, she thought.

"No, dear," she said. "Not a lot."

"And I don't look like my brothers or my sister."

"No, dear. You must take after your father."

"What was he like, Mum?"

"Tall. And dark."

"And handsome?"

"Oh, yes," said Kay.

"So when I grow up, I'll be tall, dark, and handsome, shall I, Mum?"

"Of course you will, dear," said Kay. "Of course you will."

That night as she lay in bed beside her husband, Mrs. Buzzard said thoughtfully, "What are you going to do with him, then, Ken?"

"Who?" said Farmer Buzzard sleepily.

"Smasher. Going to train him to work sheep?"

"No. He got no gift for that," said Farmer Buzzard. For he had noticed that, while the other three puppies had begun to try to herd his wife's chickens about the farmyard, Smasher had taken no part in this instinctive sheepdog behavior. His only occasional contribution had been to rush at a hen, open-mouthed, and try to grab hold of it. The farmer had not told his wife this.

"Well, what have you kept him for, then?" asked Mrs. Buzzard. "Not for his looks, surely? Come on, admit it, you've just got a soft spot for him, haven't you?"

"Not pertickerly," said Farmer Buzzard.

But he had.

It was just as well that he had, because some weeks later Smasher went looking for trouble. Not only was he growing fast, he was also getting fast on his feet, and he was starting to chase chickens in earnest. Feathers began to fly, and, fearing that blood would soon be spilled, Kay gave her son a good talking-to.

"Smasher," she said (for, hearing his name on the farmer's lips, she had learned it, just as, long ago, she had learned her own), "you are *not* to chase chickens. Do you understand?"

"Why not, Mum?"

"Because if my master catches you doing it, he will beat you."

"Why, Mum?"

"Because dogs are not allowed to chase chickens."

"Why not, Mum?"

"Because people don't like that."

"Why, Mum?"

Kay lost patience. "Oh, be quiet!" she growled. "And don't you dare say, 'Why, Mum?'" She walked away.

"Why not, Mum?" said Smasher under his breath. Chicken chasing is fun, he thought.

The next day he waited until his mother

had left the yard with the farmer to go round up the sheep. Then he went into action.

Mrs. Buzzard was making bread when she heard through the open kitchen window a

frantic chorus of shrieks and squawks. Looking out, she saw hens flapping madly everywhere as the big brown puppy galloped
clumsily among them. Some birds fluttered

into the duck pond in their panic, and after them rushed Smasher, and after *him* ran Mrs. Buzzard on her long, thin legs, a rolling pin in her floury hand and a string of angry words on her lips.

Smasher fled and Mrs. Buzzard fumed and the waterlogged hens floundered to safety.

"What d'you think your dog's been up to?" said Mrs. Buzzard when she next saw her husband.

"My dog?" said Farmer Buzzard. "She's been with me all morning."

"No, not Kay. Your puppy, that Smasher. Only chasing my chickens, that's all. Drove some of them into the duck pond and half drowned them."

"Oh," said Farmer Buzzard.

"No good you standing there saying 'Oh,'" said Mrs. Buzzard. "He wants a beating, he does, to teach him a lesson."

Farmer Buzzard went to find Smasher. No good beating him now, he thought, he won't understand what it's for. Have to catch him in the act.

Smasher was lying beside his mother in the stable with his ugly head on his paws, looking as though butter wouldn't melt in his big mouth.

"He's been a bad boy, Kay," said Farmer Buzzard softly. "You ought to have learned him better."

Then he picked up a length of rope, and with it he struck six hard blows on an old canvas tarp that was hung from the roof beam to dry.

"Naughty dog!" shouted Farmer Buzzard loudly as he whacked the tarp, while Kay and Smasher looked on in astonishment.

"Sounds like you gave *him* what for," said Mrs. Buzzard when her husband returned. "Didn't hit him too hard, I hope? He's only little."

"No," said Farmer Buzzard.

"He's a brave one, though," said his wife.

"I could hear you beating him plain as plain, yet he never made a sound."

"No," said Farmer Buzzard.

"The master sounded angry," said Smasher to his mother after Farmer Buzzard had gone.

"Yes," said Kay thoughtfully.

She looked carefully at her son. Stuck to the corner of his mouth, she could see, was a single small wet white feather.

"You've been chasing those chickens again," she said.

"Just for fun, Mum," said Smasher. "I won't do it again," he said. Or not while you're around, he thought.

"You'd better not," Kay said.

Because, she thought, puppies that chase chickens could well end up as dogs that chase sheep. And dogs that chase sheep could well end up dead.

3

As Good as Gold

Up till now, Smasher had not been allowed into the farmhouse. Once or twice he had tried to follow Kay in, but Mrs. Buzzard had always shooed him out again.

"You stay out in the stable, my lad," she had said. "You can make as much mess as you like out there."

But then she changed her mind, for two reasons. One was on account of her hens. He needs watching, that puppy does, she thought, while Ken and Kay are out around the farm. That's when he gets into mischief. Better if he's with me; then I can keep my eye on him.

The second reason was that she felt guilty. I never should have told Ken to beat him, she said to herself (and that hard too, it's not like him). After all, he's only young, even though he's growed so big. As big as his mother he is already.

So one morning, when the farmer and the collie had gone out on their rounds, Mrs. Buzzard opened the back door and called, "Smasher!" She called, had she but known it, in the nick of time, for Smasher was just about to have a go at one of her hens, which had most unwisely wandered into the stable.

Smasher, who had been dozing in the straw, lay quite still, pretending to be asleep. I'll corner this one, he thought. I know Mum said I shouldn't, but this is too good a chance to miss.

Then he heard his name called.

What a great big thing he's getting to be, thought Mrs. Buzzard as she watched him lumbering across the yard toward her. He's not gotten any better-looking, but maybe he's gotten more sensible. At least he hasn't bothered the hens lately.

She reeled as, unable to stop in time, he bumped into her legs.

"Steady!" she said. "Clumsy as an elephant." And she turned back into the house.

Smasher sat down outside the open back door. He did not expect to be invited in. He had discussed this with his mother.

"Why don't they want me in the house, Mum?" he had said.

"Because you're a yard dog," said Kay. "Not a house dog."

"But *you* go in, and you're a sheepdog, not a house dog."

"I'm both, dear," said Kay. "I know how to behave properly indoors."

So now it was with surprise that he heard Mrs. Buzzard calling, "Smasher! Come along in. Good boy."

Ears cocked, he hurried through the door and along a passage that led to the kitchen. The passageway was dark, and Smasher did not see that at one side of it there was a tall, old-fashioned umbrella stand holding a clutch of walking sticks and hung with many mackintoshes and coats and hats.

He barged straight into this, and it fell down with a great clatter. The mass of clothing enveloped him.

"Clumsy as a *herd* of elephants, I should have said!" cried Mrs. Buzzard as she put everything in order again.

While she was doing this, she heard a loud racket in the kitchen. It was Smasher upsetting a large tin basin full of water, which now streamed across the floor.

"What next!" cried Mrs. Buzzard, and her question was soon answered.

As ill luck would have it, Mrs. Buzzard was preparing to make jam that day and had put ready, on a low wooden bench close to the stove, a double rank of glass screwtop jars.

As she knelt on the kitchen floor, mopping up the water, Smasher, seeing her for the first time down at his own level, mistook her actions for some sort of game. Eagerly he bounded forward to lick her face, his long, thick tail whipping madly from side to side. Each stroke of it sent jam jars tumbling off the bench to smash to pieces on the flagstone floor.

How aptly was he named at that moment.

"Smasher!" screamed Mrs. Buzzard. "You bad dog, you!" She stood up and grabbed a mop and aimed a furious blow at the puppy, a blow that broke the remaining jam jars even as she slipped on the wet floor and fell flat on her back.

When she got to her feet once more, Smasher was nowhere to be seen.

"Only meself to blame," grumbled Mrs. Buzzard as she went down the passage to shut the back door.

"And you can stay out!" she shouted down the yard as she closed it. "Should have had more sense than to let you in in the first place."

Smasher, however, was still in the house.

Bewildered by the crash of breaking glass and the sound of Mrs. Buzzard's angry voice, he had bolted out of the kitchen through the nearest door into another of the many passageways that threaded the rambling old farmhouse. A little way along it was a small room from which a most attractive smell came to Smasher's blunt nose.

Curious, he looked into the larder and saw, upon a marble slab, a large piece of meat. Carefully, for he could still hear Mrs. Buzzard's angry voice in the distance, he took the leg of lamb in his mouth and proceeded down the passage till he came to another room.

This was Mrs. Buzzard's front parlor, a room that was her pride and joy, never used except when there was special company. It contained two large armchairs and a sofa, all upholstered in a kind of pale blue velvet, and a number of small, slender-legged tables on which stood a great many china ornaments.

Something told Smasher he had better lie low for a bit.

Earlier that morning he had been down to the duck pond for a drink, and while there had enjoyed a little paddle. His large feet (though Mrs. Buzzard had not noticed this) had on their pads a good deal of mud, mostly composed of duck muck. It had dried, but the water that had spilled on the kitchen floor had wetted it again.

Smasher padded across the room, carrying the leg of lamb. The carpet, which was of a cream color, thereby acquired a brand-new pattern. He hoisted himself up onto the sofa and tucked into the meat. This is more comfortable than the stable, he thought when only the bone was left. I'll have a nap now.

After a while Smasher woke suddenly. He felt an urgent need. He had drunk a great deal of water from the duck pond, and now he needed to get rid of some of it.

Only a few days ago he had, for the first time ever, not squatted, as all puppies do, but cocked his leg against the stable doorpost.

"Watch me, Mum," he had said. "You can't do that, can you?"

"No, I don't do that," said Kay.

Now he cocked his leg against the side of the blue velvet sofa and then, for luck, against each of the armchairs.

Handy trick, that is, he said to himself with a sigh of relief. Better than squatting in the middle of the carpet. She might not have liked that. Now then, if I'm going to be a house dog, I'd better have a good look round the place.

He wandered out of the parlor and along the passage till he came to the foot of a flight of stairs. Up these Smasher climbed, and saw, facing the head of the stairs, an open bedroom door. In he went.

It was the Buzzards' bedroom, and on the Buzzards' bed, as yet unmade, was a candlewick bedspread, fringed with rows of little round bobbles. After trying unsuccessfully to jump up on the bed, Smasher contented himself with chewing off a great many of the bobbles.

Then he turned his attention to the bottom of the curtains and altered their shape a good deal. Then he found Mrs. Buzzard's slippers and chewed up the left one. Then he came across Farmer Buzzard's slippers and chewed up one of those (the right one, as it happened).

After that, bored with chewing things,

Smasher decided to go downstairs again. They were quite steep, and he fell most of the way.

Passing the parlor door once more, he looked in and there, on the sofa, sniffing at the lamb bone—*his* lamb bone—was one of Mrs. Buzzard's cats.

Furiously, Smasher rushed at it, overturning a couple of little tables on his way into the room and another couple on his way out after the fleeing cat, while china ornaments flew everywhere.

Out through the back door went the cat,

for the door was now open again, Mrs. Buzzard having left it so while she went down to the yard to make sure that Smasher wasn't after her hens.

Smasher followed, but the cat was much too quick for him, and he gave up the chase. He made his way to the stable and lay down, full of lamb and tired out by his morning's work.

A few minutes later, Mrs. Buzzard looked in and saw him lying there.

"Bless him," she said as she made her way back to the farmhouse. "There's me thinking the worst of him, and all the time he's lying there as good as gold."

In the kitchen she looked up at the clock on the wall and said, "Now then, I must make the bed and dust the front parlor, and then I'll put that nice leg of lamb on to cook."

4

The Field Barn

"And on top of all that," said Mrs. Buzzard, "he wetted on my three-piece suite!"

She had just finished detailing to her husband the damage done by the puppy. *His* puppy.

"Add it all together," she said, "and you're looking at a hundred pounds' worth and more. You named him well, you did."

"Oh," said Farmer Buzzard.

"No good you standing there saying 'Oh,'" replied Mrs. Buzzard. "What are you going to do about it, that's what I'm asking."

"Dunno."

"Well, I do. That animal is never coming inside my house again. Never. Which I dare say he'll try to do unless I keeps every door shut from now on. Which I'm not prepared to do, this fine weather. So there's only one answer."

"What's that, Martha?" said Farmer Buzzard.

"You got to get rid of him."

"Sell him, you mean?"

"Don't know about *sell* him," said Mrs. Buzzard. "Nobody would buy such an ugly creature, not unless 'twas a half-blind man."

"You surely don't mean," said Farmer Buzzard, "that you want me to..." He stopped, unable to complete the sentence.

"I don't care what you does, Ken," said Mrs. Buzzard, "just so long as he's gone. After today, I never wants to set eyes on him again."

Meanwhile, in the stable, Smasher was saying, "Guess what, Mum."

"What, dear?"

"I think I'm going to be a house dog. I was invited into the house today."

"Did you enjoy it?"

"Oh, yes!" said Smasher. "It was smashing."

"I hope you behaved yourself," said Kay.

At that moment they saw the farmer coming across the yard toward them. He carried his gun in the crook of his arm.

He picked up the length of rope with which he had once whacked the tarp, and tied it round Smasher's neck. Then he set off with the two dogs, Smasher cavorting excitedly on the end of the rope, Kay trotting soberly at heel. Out through the yard gate they went and off across the fields.

Sometime afterward, Mrs. Buzzard, sitting at her sewing machine repairing her tattered bedroom curtains, heard the bang of a distant gun.

"Oh, no!" she said. "He's surely not gone and..." She stopped, unable to complete the sentence.

"I heard a shot," she said when her husband returned.

"Rabbit," said Farmer Buzzard. "Missed him."

That evening, Mrs. Buzzard had no cause to go into the stable. But if she had, she would have found Kay there alone.

So busy was Mrs. Buzzard with curtain mending, and bedspread mending, and the cleaning of carpet and furniture, and the repair of broken ornaments, and the collecting of replacement jam jars, that it was not until twenty-four hours later that she found time to say, "That Smasher. What have you done with him?"

"Found him a good home," said Farmer Buzzard.

"That's quick, then," said Mrs. Buzzard with relief. "Difficult, was it, to place him?"

"Not pertickerly," said Farmer Buzzard.

At the far end of the farm there stood, in the middle of a field, an old stone barn with a walled yard in front of it. Here, in winter, Farmer Buzzard kept a dozen or so cattle.

Now it contained one animal only—Smasher.

This was where the farmer had gone the previous day, gun in hand, one dog at heel, the other on a rope, while slung across his back was his game bag. In it was a feeding dish and a supply of dog food. When they reached the field barn, Farmer Buzzard shut the gate of the yard behind them and let Smasher off the rope.

He checked that there were some straw bales inside the building, that the cattle trough was low enough for Smasher to drink from, and that the bars of the gate were too close together for him to squeeze between. The walls were too high to be jumped.

It was a prison, certainly, but a roomy and comfortable one nevertheless, and a perfect hiding place. No one ever came there but the farmer. No one would know. Mrs. Buzzard certainly wouldn't.

Farmer Buzzard sat down on a bale of straw, and Smasher bumbled up and shoved his wrinkled face into his master's lap.

Farmer Buzzard did his best to explain the situation.

"Now you listen here, my boy," he said, "while I puts you in the picture. You've blotted your copybook proper, you have, and my missus wants to see the back of you for good and all. She'd like me to take you to the pound, I daresay. Or worse. Which I'm not going to do. And why not? Because I've growed fond of you, ugly and clumsy and destructive as you are. There's good in you somewheres, I'm sure of it. So you've got to stay here whether you likes it or not. Your mum and me, we'll come and visit you every day, to exercise you and to feed you, while we give things time to settle down at home."

"What was all that about, Mum?" asked Smasher as the farmer stood up and, cutting the strings of the bale he'd been sitting on, began to strew it about to make a bed.

Kay had not, of course, understood Farmer Buzzard's actual words, but she knew instinctively what was going to happen. Smasher, for some reason, was going to be kept down here in the field barn for the time being. He must have done something wrong. He's in the doghouse, she thought to herself.

"I think, dear," she said, "that the master was telling you that now you're a big boy— not a puppy anymore but a dog—and he's giving you your very own place to live. See, he's brought your feeding dish and he's going to give you your supper now, and a lovely supper it looks."

Farmer Buzzard put the loaded feeding dish down on the floor, and Smasher dug in.

Quietly the farmer said, "Come, Kay," and quickly they slipped out of the barn, through the yard, and out the gate, which Farmer Buzzard latched behind them.

It's only for a few days, he said to himself as they walked home. Till the storm blows over.

But all the same he was worried at the thought of the dog left all alone, so much so that when a rabbit popped up right in front of them, he completely missed his shot.

When Smasher had finished his food, he went to the gate, through which, his nose told him, his mother and the master had gone. But it was closed. He tried to squeeze between the bars, but he was too big.

Oh, well, he thought, they'll be back in a minute. He was quite used to being on his own during the daytime, in the stable. He had a drink at the cattle trough, went into the barn, lay down on his straw bed, and went to sleep.

When he woke again, it was getting dark, and still they hadn't come back. Mum's always back by dark, he thought. Never in his short life had Smasher slept a night on his own.

He went to the gate again and looked out, but there was nothing to be seen except the distant lights of the farmhouse.

That's where I should be if I'm going to be a house dog, thought Smasher. Not stuck out here. And he pointed his blunt snout at the sky and let out a long, doleful howl.

In the stable Kay heard it. Poor boy, she thought. He's lonely.

In the house Mrs. Buzzard heard it.

"What's that?" she said.

"Dog howling somewhere," said Farmer Buzzard.

"Not Kay, is it?"

"No, she's in the stable."

"Well, it can't be that Smasher," said Mrs. Buzzard. "He's in his new home, I'm thankful to say. He'll soon settle down there."

"I hopes," said Farmer Buzzard.

5

A Stifled Sneeze

Only for a few days, Farmer Buzzard had said to himself. But two months later, Smasher was still living in the field barn.

The more he thought about it, the more the farmer was sure that there was no point in bringing the dog back to the farm yet, much less in hoping that Smasher would be allowed in the house again.

Mrs. Buzzard's wounds were too raw— she would never allow it.

The return could only possibly happen when Smasher was a fully trained animal.

"So," said Farmer Buzzard to Kay, "we must set about training this son of yours. He must have some of your brains, whoever his father was. And he's anxious to please, which is half the battle."

On this last point he was right. Smasher was indeed keen to be in the farmer's good graces. When, after that first evening, his mother told him that howling at night (or at any other time) was not a good idea, he did not howl again.

At first he thought of the field barn as a prison, but as time went on, and Kay kept telling him how lucky he was to have such a place all to himself, Smasher began first to accept and then to quite enjoy his solitary life.

Nor was it all that solitary, for the master came with Kay three times every day. They came in the morning, on their rounds of the sheep and cattle, and again in the evening, when Smasher was fed. And in the middle of each day, in the early afternoon, Farmer Buzzard set aside a couple of hours for a training session.

He was by nature a good trainer of dogs, knowledgeable and firm and, above all, patient. He was determined that this ugly dog of his should become a model pupil. Tearing things up and wetting in the house was puppy stuff, never to be repeated.

To put the dog's teeth to proper use, he gave Smasher big marrow bones to gnaw. But the wetting was a more difficult problem. The only way open to him, Farmer Buzzard decided, was to pretend that the field barn was a house and teach Smasher to do everything he had to do in the yard outside. Barn-trained equaled house-trained, he reckoned.

It took time, because Smasher couldn't see the point of it, but Kay encouraged him and the farmer rewarded him, and soon it became habit.

In the meantime Smasher was taken around the farm (always out of sight of the house) on a leash and taught to walk at heel.

Then, off the leash, he was taught to sit, and at the command "Down!" to lie down, and at "Stay!" to remain lying down, even when the master moved away from him. At first Farmer Buzzard only took a few steps away, but before too long he could walk halfway across a field and stop and look back to see Smasher still lying where he had been put.

After the earlier business with the chickens, Farmer Buzzard was concerned that Smasher might chase the cattle, or worse, the sheep. But he need not have worried. Smasher showed no interest in either.

The credit for this was Kay's.

The very first time that Smasher had gone amongst the flock of sheep while off the leash, he had made a little rush at a lamb when the farmer's back was turned. Farmer Buzzard looked round at the sound of a sudden growl followed by a sharp yelp of pain, to see Smasher holding up a paw and looking very sorry for himself. Kay, he saw, had her hackles up.

Perhaps he trod on her, Farmer Buzzard thought. He's clumsy enough and a lot bigger than her, too.

"What's up, Kay?" he said, but she could not, of course, answer.

"Ow!" cried Smasher. "That hurt, Mum! What did you want to do that for?"

"To teach you a lesson, I hope," said Kay angrily. "I told you before what happens to dogs who chase sheep. I never want to see you chasing an animal on this farm again, ever, whether it's chickens or bullocks or sheep, do you understand?"

"Yes, Mum," said Smasher, licking his bitten paw.

"You're doing very well in your training," said Kay, "so don't go messing it up now. Say to yourself, whatever happens, I must always act sensibly."

"Yes, Mum," said Smasher. "If I do, d'you

think I'll be a house dog in the end?"

"I don't know," said Kay.

She looked up at the farmer and whined a little, which meant "D'you think he will be?" But the farmer could not, of course, answer.

When two months had gone by, a major problem arose.

The time was fast approaching when Farmer Buzzard would need the field barn and yard to house a dozen bullocks through the winter months. Then there would be no way that Smasher could stay. He might be barn-trained, but the bullocks certainly weren't.

"I got no choice," said the farmer to Kay. "He'll have to come back up to the farm. Can't take him in the house, Martha won't have it, but she might just put up with him being in the stable again. After all, time's passed since he did all that damage, and what's more, he's well-trained now."

Farmer Buzzard left things as late as he could. But it had been a wet autumn, and already the heavy bullocks were beginning to tread the fields, especially around the gateways and water troughs, into a muddy mess.

"Anyways," he said to Kay, "with the cold weather coming, we can't leave Smasher down here all through the winter. He needs to come in by the fire nighttimes, like you do."

Accordingly he determined that the following Saturday he would yard the bullocks and bring Smasher back to the farm.

He did not try to prepare the way for this by any mention of his plans to his wife. She, after all, believed that the dog had been living with a new master for almost three months now.

"We'll just have to take a chance," he said to Smasher. "One thing's certain, I'm not getting rid of you." And he patted his ugly brown dog.

As he did so, it struck him how much Smasher had grown—what a big, strong animal he now was—and he remembered the words of his neighbor who had bought Smasher's sister.

"He's more like a bull-mastiff than a collie," he had said.

"You *are*, too," Farmer Buzzard said now. "And as for ugly, well, I don't know so much about that. Maybe I've just got used to the way you look, with that wrinkly pushed-in face of yours, but I wouldn't call you ugly. True, you're not as handsome as some. But all the same you've growed into a fine strong dog. You look—what's the word I want?— noble. Yes, that's it. Noble."

On the Saturday that he was going to yard the bullocks, Farmer Buzzard said to Smasher, "You don't know it, my son, but you'll be spending this night in the stable."

What Farmer Buzzard did not know was that Smasher would be spending that night in the farmhouse.

Fate, in the shape of another dog, took a hand in the matter.

Just as the farmer was about to set off with Kay to take the bullocks down to the field barn, the phone rang.

Mrs. Buzzard answered it.

"Yes?" she said. "Oh, no! Oh, dear, oh, dear! Oh, yes. Of course. Yes. No. Yes. No. Straightaway."

"What was all that about, Martha?" asked her husband.

"That was our Bertha," said Mrs. Buzzard.

Mrs. Buzzard's unmarried sister Bertha lived in the nearby town, alone save for her dog, a much-spoiled Pekingese.

"That May-Wong of hers," Mrs. Buzzard went on, "tripped her up and she fell down the stairs. Nothing broken, doctor says, but she's ever so bruised and she wants me to come for a few days and look after her. You could manage, couldn't you, Ken?"

"I daresay," replied Farmer Buzzard.

"You'll have Kay for company."

Not only Kay, thought the farmer.

"You don't mind, then?"

"Not pertickerly," said Farmer Buzzard.

That evening, after Mrs. Buzzard had gone to her sister's and the bullocks were safely yarded down at the field barn, Farmer Buzzard sat comfortably in his favorite chair, watching the telly. At his feet lay his dogs.

Farmer Buzzard enjoyed television. Recently he had treated himself to a brand-new set, the latest model, with a very big screen.

When it arrived, Mrs. Buzzard had said, "You want to put a rug over that thing night-times."

"Whatever for?" said Farmer Buzzard.

"Burglars," said Mrs. Buzzard. "There's been a lot of it about, breaking into people's houses and taking their tellies and video recorders and that. They look through the window and see that great big thing, they'll take it."

"That's in town," said Farmer Buzzard. "They don't come out here."

Now, at bedtime, he pointed the remote control at his pride and joy and switched it off.

Then he put the dogs out for a run.

Then he shut Kay up in the stable.

"I hopes your feelings won't be hurt, old girl," he said. "But I want Smasher to be on his own in the house for the night. If he's going to do anything naughty, it's better done while Martha's away."

Inside the house, he put an old blanket on the floor beside his chair and made Smasher lie down on it.

"Now, you be a good boy," he said.

"You're not a pup anymore, you're a dog, so you behave yourself." And he climbed the stairs to bed.

This is the life, thought Smasher drowsily. At last I'm a house dog. And he fell happily asleep.

He slept so soundly that he did not hear stealthy footsteps outside the window in the

middle of the night. Nor did he hear the slight scraping noise as the window was expertly forced. What woke him was in fact, a stifled sneeze.

The burglar had shone his flashlight upon the television set and had just unplugged it when he felt the sneeze coming on. He hastily pressed a forefinger above his upper lip.

For a moment he stood stock-still, listening in case the slight noise had woken anyone upstairs. But then *he* heard a slight noise.

Turning round, he shone his flashlight, and there, standing directly between him and the open window, was the biggest, ugliest dog he had ever seen.

6
New Dog

Hullo, said Smasher to himself, who's this, then? Must be a pal of the master's, come to stay. Being a friendly dog, he advanced toward the man, tail wagging, ugly mouth agape in what was actually a smile but looked in the dim light like an angry snarl.

"Good dog," whispered the burglar in a shaky voice. Smasher, encouraged by this, leapt up and put his large paws on the man's chest.

The burglar was a small man, and he fell backward under the weight of the dog. He began to shout, "No! No! Get him off me! Help!"

Good game, this, Smasher thought, and he began to bark loudly with excitement.

Woken by the hubbub, Farmer Buzzard hurried downstairs, snatching his gun from its cupboard on the way. He opened the door of the room and switched on the lights to see Smasher standing on the man's chest and giving his face a thorough washing with his large, slobbery tongue, while the burglar still cried, indistinctly now, for help. Farmer Buzzard looked at the open window and then at the unplugged television set.

Martha was right, he thought.

He pointed to Smasher's blanket and said, "Down!" Smasher obeyed. Then he waved his gun toward the prostrate burglar and said, "And you stay down, too, or my dog'll tear your throat out."

Then he rang the police.

"The master was ever so pleased with me, Mum," said Smasher to Kay when they met the next morning.

"What happened, dear?" asked Kay. "I heard you barking in the middle of the night, and then later on I heard a car drive up, and then voices. What was it?"

"I don't really know, Mum," said Smasher. "A man came and I thought he was a friend of the master's and I had a bit of a game with him. But then some other men came, dressed in blue and wearing funny hats, and they took him away in a car with his hands sort of tied together."

"Handcuffs," said Kay. "Policemen. He must have been a burglar. He came to steal something, and you stopped him, dear!" And, just as her master had done, she said, warmly, "*What* a good boy!"

One evening, a week later, Mrs. Buzzard returned. She found her husband sitting watching the telly, the remote control in his hand, the collie at his feet. In the next room there was, though she did not know it, another dog, lying still and silent, as he had been told to do.

"Well, Ken," she said, kissing the top of his head. "You been all right?"

Farmer Buzzard nodded.

Conversation was not possible with him, Mrs. Buzzard knew, while he was watching television. So she waited until the program had ended and then said, "Everything been all right here?"

Farmer Buzzard switched off the television.

"You were right, Martha," he said.

"What about?"

"Burglars. We had one, the first night you was away."

"No!"

"Yes. After my telly, he was."

"I told you!" Mrs. Buzzard said. "I said you ought to cover it up nighttimes. But he didn't get it, then?"

"No," said Farmer Buzzard.

"You caught him?"

"No. My dog caught him."

"Oh, Kay!" cried Mrs. Buzzard. "*What* a good dog!" And she bent to stroke the collie.

"No, not Kay," said her husband. "My new dog."

"New dog?"

"Yes. The very day you went to Bertha's, it was. After what you said about burglars, I thought to meself, what we need is a proper house dog, a big, strong animal that will guard the place, one that no burglar would face."

"So you went out and got one?"

"I went out," said Farmer Buzzard truthfully, "and I got one. And by the time I got downstairs that night, he'd knocked the burglar down and he was standing on him. 'He'll tear your throat out,' I said to the man. We needn't worry about burglars anymore."

"Well, I never!" said Mrs. Buzzard. "Where is he, then, this new dog?"

For answer Farmer Buzzard stood up and opened the connecting door. "Come!" he said. In walked Smasher.

"Sit!" said the farmer, and he sat.

"Down!" said the farmer, and he lay down, tail gently wagging, a big grin on his wrinkly pushed-in face.

"He won't tear my throat out, will he?" said Mrs. Buzzard, a trifle nervously.

Farmer Buzzard laughed.

"Never!" he said. "He's a soft old thing, he is."

Like you, thought Mrs. Buzzard.

"It's a funny thing," she said, "but I tell you who he reminds me of. I know I haven't got my proper spectacles on, but he puts me in a mind of that puppy we got rid of. You know, the one that did all that damage. That Smasher."

"That's what I call this dog, too," said Farmer Buzzard.

"You're right, he is a big, strong dog," said Mrs. Buzzard. "We'll be all right with him in the house. Though he's no beauty, mind. How would you describe him? What's the word?"

"Noble," said her husband.

Mrs. Buzzard nodded.

"But doesn't he remind you of that ugly puppy too?" she asked.

"Not pertickerly," said Farmer Buzzard.

About the Author

Dick King-Smith was born and raised in Gloucestershire, England. After twenty years as a farmer, he turned to teaching and then to writing the children's books that have earned him critical acclaim on both sides of the Atlantic. Mr. King-Smith is the author of numerous books for children, including *Babe: The Gallant Pig*, which was made into an award-winning major motion picture.